SHEEPISH RIDDLES

Katy Hall and Lisa Eisenberg

pictures by R. W. Alley

Dial easy-to-read

Dial Books for Young Readers   New York

Published by Dial Books for Young Readers
A Division of Penguin Books USA Inc.
375 Hudson Street
New York, New York 10014

Text copyright © 1996 by Katy Hall and Lisa Eisenberg
Pictures copyright © 1996 by R. W. Alley
Printed in Hong Kong

The Dial Easy-to-Read logo is a registered trademark of
Dial Books for Young Readers,
A Division of Penguin Books USA Inc.,
® TM 1,162,718.

First Edition
1 3 5 7 9 10 8 6 4 2

Library of Congress Cataloging in Publication Data
Hall, Katy.
Sheepish riddles / by Katy Hall and Lisa Eisenberg; pictures by R. W. Alley.
—1st ed.   p.   cm.
ISBN 0-8037-1535-8—ISBN 0-8037-1536-6 (library)
1. Riddles, Juvenile. 2. Sheep—Juvenile humor. [1. Riddles.
2. Jokes. 3. Sheep—Wit and humor.] I. Eisenberg, Lisa.
II. Alley, Robert, ill. III. Title.
PN6371.5.H3487 1996 818'.5402—dc20 93-32212 CIP AC

*The paintings, which consist of black ink and watercolors,
are color-separated and reproduced in full color.*

Reading Level 2.1

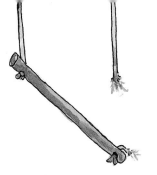

To Baabra Streisand
K.H. and L.E.

To Cassandra and Max,
who increasingly "get it"
R.W.A.

Where do sheep go
to get a haircut?

To the baa-baa shop!

What do polite lambs say
to their mothers?

Thank ewe!

8

What would you get
if you crossed a sheep
with an elephant?

A *wool*-ly mammoth!

What kind of sheep can jump
higher than a house?

Any kind!
Houses can't jump!

What time is it
when a dozen wolves
are chasing a sheep?

Twelve after one!

What movies are sheep
lining up to see?

Baaaatman!

What would you get
if you crossed
a sheep and a bee?

A baa humbug!

What did the sheep
say to the grass?

It's been nice gnawing you!

What were the sheep
doing on the highway?

Oh, about two miles an hour!

Why are sheep famous?

They are out standing
in their field!

How many sheep
were born last year?

None!
Only lambs were born!

How did Little Bo Peep
lose her sheep?

She had a crook with her!

What do sheep do
when they can't sleep?

They count people!

What's the most important use for sheepskin?

To hold the sheep together!

STEERING WHEEL COVER?

WRONG!

BOOTS?

WRONG!

HAT?

WRONG!

DIPLOMA?

BIG HORN EWENIVERSITY

YOU HAVE GRADUATED!

WRONG, AGAIN!

What would you get
if you crossed a lamb
with a cocker spaniel?

A sheepdog!

What did Cinderella Sheep
lose at the ball?

Her *grass* slipper!

What would you get
if you taught a little sheep
to do karate?

Lamb chops!

What did the ram say
to the ewe?

Wool you marry me?

What do you get
if you cross a sheep and
a piece of chocolate?

A candy baa!

What do you get if you cross
a baby sheep and a firefly?

A lamb with
night vision!

What do you get if you cross
a sheep and a vampire?

A wool coat that
sticks to your neck!

How can you tell
when sheep like a movie?

They all *flock* to see it!

What do you get if you cross
a sheepherder and a ghost?

Little Boo Peep!

Why is it hard
to talk to a ram?

He keeps butting in!

What do sheep think about haircuts?

They think they're
shear nonsense!

What did the sheep do
when she lost her wool?

She knit her brow!

What kind of story
do little lambs like?

A long yarn!

What is a sheep's
favorite tale?

Ali Baaa Baaa
and the 40 Thieves!

What song do little lambs like?

"On the Good Sheep Lollipop!"

Why did the sheep
keep going straight down
the road?

No ewe turns
were permitted!

What kind of birthday party
do lambs like?

Sheepovers!

What do you get if you cross a thief and a sheep?

Steal wool!

Who is a sheep's
favorite tough guy?

Ram-bo!

What do you get if you cross
a sheep and a bucket of sand?

Knitty gritty!

What did the lamb say
to the blanket?

Is that you, Mama?

Why did the man
carry his sheep across
his frozen pond?

He didn't want anyone pulling
the wool over his ice!

What does a sheep say
when it has a cold?

Baa-choo!

What do you get when you
have a father sheep, a baby
sheep, and a doorbell?

A rama-*lamb*-a-ding-dong!

44

What West Coast town
do sheep come from?

Santa Baa-baa!

What's a sheep's
favorite painting?

The Mona Fleesa!

What do you get if you cross
a field with a sheep?

To the other side!

What kind of sheep goes "Beeeeeeep! BEEEEEEEP! *BEEEEEEEP!*"

A big*horn* sheep!

48